BOB & BARRY'S LUNAR ADVENTURES

SIMON
BARTRAM

templar publishing
www.templarco.co.uk

IDENTITY CARD

Name: **Bob**

Occupation: **Man on the Moon**

Licence to Drive: **Space rocket**

Planet of residence: **Earth**

Alien activity: **non-aware**

WORLDWIDE ASTRONAUT'S ASSOCIATION

CHAPTER ONE

"Come on," said Bob, the Man on the Moon, to his best-ever friend, Barry the six-legged dog. "Let's get a wriggle on! The clocks a-ticking!"

As usual, Bob had been hard at work all day, looking after the Moon – clearing up space litter, entertaining visitors, sweeping out craters and checking for aliens. Though of course, Bob, like any other sensible person, knows that there are no such things as aliens.

For once Bob was keen to leave work early and so had slightly shortened his Moon-themed variety show. Luckily, the space tourists didn't really mind missing his famous space chimp impressions as they too were eager to get back to Earth quick-sharp. It was going to be a special night. The STUPENDOUS ALACAZAMO was coming to town!!

Across the globe, the Stupendous Alacazamo was the most famous magician ever to sport a top hat and cape. Bob had only been seven when he'd first watched him on TV. With a single wave of his wand, Alacazamo miraculously transformed an ordinary free-range chicken into a mighty African elephant. Bob's eyes had almost popped out of his head. He'd been hooked ever since. Finally tonight he was about to see Alacazamo's spectacular live show. He was so excited he could hardly fly his rocket straight.

Having landed back at the Lunar Hill launch-pad, Bob quickly popped into his changing cubicle. In a super-fast flash, he shoved on his Earth clothes and cycled home as quickly as his legs would take him. It wasn't until later that he realised he hadn't put on his vest.

At home, after a speedy wash and brush-up, he wolfed down some fish-paste sandwiches and selected his favourite mesmerising swirl badge to wear.

"Perfect!" he beamed.

Bob then dug out the precious tickets that were hidden in an old biscuit tin between the sheets in the airing cupboard. He'd saved for months to buy them and had even sold his third-best tank top to raise some extra money.

"Nights out don't come cheap, Barry," he said. "Especially if you fancy getting a souvenir T-shirt or a choc-ice."

It was almost time to set off. All Bob had to do was find his autograph book and set his trusty old video to record the football.

The streets outside were buzzing. It seemed as if the whole town was off to see the show. The Moon shone brightly overhead as Bob and Barry set off down the road. As the Glitterball Theatre came into view, butterflies began to swirl around Bob's tummy. His legs wobbled as he walked through the theatre's grand, pillared entrance and into the beautiful auditorium.

He and Barry were the first to take their seats, but soon the theatre filled up around them. Then, at eight o'clock, the lights dimmed. A huge cheer filled the auditorium before it was replaced by an electric hush. In the darkness a thousand eyes could just make out the heavy, velvet curtains swishing open. Bob's heart was racing. Suddenly, a tremendous bang and a flash of lightning made the whole audience jump. A hundred spotlights cut through the darkness and revealed a cloud of smoke swirling around the stage. The audience "OOOHED!" and "AAAHED!" as the silhouette of a caped figure began to emerge through the haze.

For Bob it was a dream come true. In front of his very eyes, there he was at last...

CHAPTER TWO

"UNBELIEVABLE!" shouted Cornelius Trolley.

"ASTOUNDING!" agreed Harriet Song.

"MAGIC!" cheered Bob.

From the very first zap of his wand, the Stupendous Alacazamo had his fans spellbound. The show had rope tricks and card tricks and cup tricks. It had jaw-dropping escapology and mind-blowing levitation. It whizz-popped and shimmered and snap-cracked and glimmered. All night, delighted audience members helped out with the wizardry. Superstar footballer Archibald Chumley was hypnotised into thinking he was a helicopter. The Reverend Pips' toupee was brought to life and it glided round the theatre like a bald eagle. And to the horror of the watching children, tyrant headmaster Clement Twit was cloned.

Later, as the Stupendous Alacazamo began to saw Edna Kipperbeard in two, the chap next to Bob started to look awfully queasy. He'd turned green and could only watch the show through one eye.

"She'll be fine!" whispered Bob. "He's only mucked this trick up once before, when he was practising on a custard slice!"

Sure enough, Edna Kipperbeard sprang from the stage in one piece and without a trace of glue or sticky tape on her.

And so the show went on. By ten-thirty the Stupendous Alacazamo had one more chunk of wonder up his sleeve.

"For my Grand Finale," he announced, "I shall perform a feat of magic the like of which has never been attempted before. LADIES AND GENTLEMEN, PREPARE TO BE AMAZED AS I, THE STUPENDOUS ALACAZAMO, DISAPPEAR THE MOON!!!!"

The smile dropped from Bob's face. All around, gasps could be heard as everything went black. A few tense moments passed until, out of the gloom, a massive projection of the golden Moon flashed up onto the stage backdrop. Everybody struggled to adjust to its

brightness, but when they did they were utterly amazed. The Stupendous Alacazamo was flying, high above the audience, swooping and soaring like the Reverend Pips' toupee. Then, he turned in the air and jetted towards the Moon projection with the speed of a superhero. Faster and faster he flew... until... KABOOM!... he was lost in a flash of blinding light. The audience screamed as the Moon projection vanished under a smoky darkness. Silence fell upon the theatre. Then, a booming voice startled everyone.

"PEOPLE OF THE WORLD, BEHOLD MY GENIUS! LEAVE NOW AND LOOK TO THE SKIES! MY WORK HERE IS DONE. I BID YOU GOOD NIGHT!"

With that, the lights came up and the magician was nowhere to be seen. Everyone rushed outside. Owls were hooting and the stars were twinkling in the clear night sky. Everything was normal – apart from one thing.

"UNBELIEVABLE!" shouted Gilbert Giblet.

"ASTOUNDING!" cried Matilda Boilankle.

"MAGIC!" cheered Horace Hockney-Fudge.

Only Bob and Barry stood quietly amongst all the applause. As they looked upwards their eyes met a strange emptiness in the sky. Their beloved Moon was nowhere to be seen. It had completely and utterly disappeared.

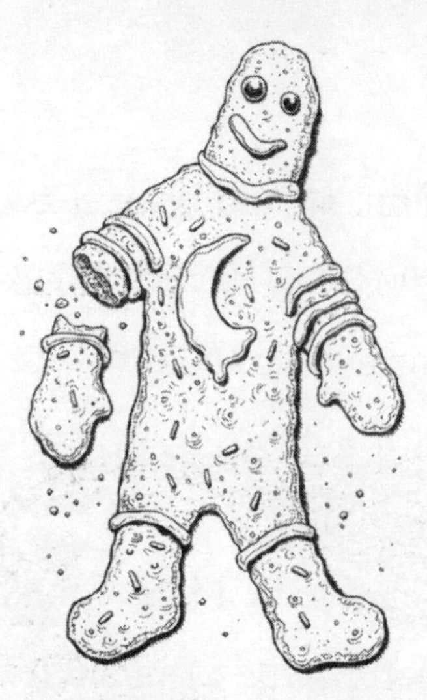

CHAPTER THREE

That night, Bob tossed and turned, dreaming of deserted skies that were blacker than black. At 4.23 a.m. he woke and couldn't drift off to sleep again, so he went downstairs to bake gingerbread astronauts. His head was full of so many thoughts.

He knew that every month the Moon looked thinner and thinner, until you couldn't actually see it, but it was still up there, orbiting the Earth. *It couldn't just vanish in a second though, could it? Perhaps it had been a trick of the light, rather than a trick of the Stupendous Alacazamo.*

In the end, Bob convinced himself that there was absolutely nothing to worry about and, by the time the sun rose at 6.23 a.m., so had his spirits.

"Come on, Barry, old pal," he chirped. "Shake a leg! We've mucho mooning to do today!"

So, after a breakfast of kippers and star-shaped toast for Bob, and a selection of bones for Barry, they were soon blasting upwards through space. As usual, Bob popped his rocket onto autopilot to spend the fifteen-minute journey reading *The Daily Bugle*.

"Hey, Barry," he laughed. "Listen to this – there's a lad called Albert Snodgrass who's convinced that his pet cat, Barbara, is some kind of alien. What a complete fruit loop *he* must be!"

Barry groaned quietly – Bob had never

seemed to notice that he was a slightly *unusual* looking dog, who actually came from the planet Zootron 6.

After that, Bob read the football reports, the weather forecast and the cartoon strips. In truth, he was desperate to avoid the main headline. He couldn't for long. It was too big and too loud.

"ALACAZA-NO-MOON!!" it shouted. "ASTONISHING LUNAR-LOSS SHOCK!"

Page after page detailed the strange events of the previous evening.

"We'll prove 'em wrong," chuckled Bob. "By tonight Barbara the extra-terrestrial cat will be the lead story. Guaranteed. We'll be on the Moon in a matter of minutes."

But, a couple of those minutes passed, and then a couple more, without the Moon coming into view.

"How very strange!" said Bob, tapping the

dials on his control panel. "The Moon should be right there." He flicked some switches and pressed some buttons. "Hmmm! We obviously have a navigation thingymabob malfunction problemo! We'll just have to keep our eyes peeled. It's got to be around here somewhere!"

But it wasn't. The golden Moon was nowhere to be seen.

"Oh, Barry," gasped Bob, "I think… I think… *The Daily Bugle* might be right! The Stupendous Alacazamo has ACTUALLY done it. He's DISAPPEARED THE MOON!! WHAT ON *EARTH* ARE WE GOING TO DO NOW?"

CHAPTER FOUR

"A LOVELY CUP OF TEA!" thought Bob. "That's the answer to every problem."

But not that morning. By nine-fifteen he had slurped and sipped his way through his whole flask and he was more befuddled than ever. Eventually, he decided that the best plan for now would be to head home.

Back on Earth, Bob locked up his spaceship on Lunar Hill launch-pad and went to take off his spacesuit. As he trudged into his changing cubicle, he noticed an official-looking letter that had been pushed under the door. Nervously, Bob ripped it open and read…

O.M.A.

BOB,
YOU ARE REQUESTED
TO REPORT TO
INFINITY HOUSE AT
1500 HOURS SHARP ON
A MATTER OF UTMOST
IMPORTANCE. DO
NOT BE LATE!

T. Van Trumpet

P.S. BRING CAKE.
P.P.S. NOT FRUIT CAKE!

It was signed by Tarantula Van Trumpet, Head of the Department for Moon Affairs. Bob gulped. So did Barry. Standing on Puddle Lane, between the library and the laundrette, Infinity House was the headquarters for the entire universe. Spacemen were hardly ever summoned there to hear good news.

After changing, Bob swiftly cycled to Vera Crumble's bakery to carefully choose a cake.

"Fingers crossed, a Victoria sponge should do the trick," he hoped.

At Infinity House, Bob was shown through a brown door into a brown office on the seventeenth floor where Tarantula Van Trumpet

was busy doodling skulls on his notepad. He didn't look up as he spoke.

"I'm sorry-ish to inform you," he said, "that the disappearance of the Moon has put us… or rather you… in a most difficult position. If there is no Moon then, unfortunately – for you, that is – we shall no longer have a need for a Man on the Moon. You have one week from tomorrow to find it. Should you fail, then I'm afraid you will have to find yourself a job elsewhere. Now please leave cake and close the door behind you. Good day!"

Bob was stunned. It most certainly *wasn't* a good day. The thought of not being the Man on the Moon saddened him down to his bones.

"I don't want to do anything else!" he cried. "I'm no good at anything else!"

Back on the street, Bob sat quietly on a bench with Barry beside him and watched the Sun set behind the cityscape. As he feared, no Moon replaced it. The words "ONE WEEK," bounced around his brain. He had to find the Moon. He JUST HAD TO!

CHAPTER FIVE

That evening Bob was in no mood to attend his bagpipes lesson. His mind was racing. Had the Moon actually vanished or had it just been moved? Had it ever been lost before? Could he find it in a week? Where on earth was the tin opener? There were so many questions, but very few answers.

"We'll just have to search every inch of the universe," said Bob. "It's bound to turn up. After all, it's pretty big and let's face facts, if trophies were handed out for spotting stuff, my sideboard would be crammed full of them."

Barry rolled his eye and scratched his ear with one of his six legs.

Of course, the Moon *was* big, but the universe was bigger. Bob wasn't quite sure exactly how much bigger but he was confident that he could get around it in six-ish days, if he didn't hang about. Even so, there was a lot of preparation to do.

First he made ninety-nine fish-paste sandwiches, before nipping out to the newsagent to buy four small batteries to power his rocket. Two might've been enough, but he was taking no chances. He didn't want to conk out on the dark side of Pluto again.

When Bob returned, he spent ten minutes doing eye exercises. First he winked, then he blinked and finally he stared for a bit, mainly at his football. It was essential training for serious Moon-spotting.

He then did three and a half press-ups, four star jumps and a squat thrust. He would have done more, but he still had to check his 'STUFF TO REMEMBER' list.

"Let's see, now," he said, reading the list, "space atlas, super-strength binoculars, passport, toiletries, spare undies, ten-piece Jupiter jigsaw and bagpipes. All present and correct!"

The bagpipes were a late addition. He hoped to find the odd minute to practise. The Christmas concert was getting closer all the time.

With everything ready, Bob and Barry watched the recorded football highlights and then went to their beds. For a second night Bob dreamed of empty skies and for a second morning, he was up before the Sun.

As the world still slept, Bob and Barry cycled towards the Lunar Hill launch-pad, where Bob put the fish paste sandwiches and some assorted bones for Barry in the rocket's mini-fridge. Then he fitted two of the new batteries into the panel under the dashboard. Now they were ready.

Bob took a deep breath and counted down…

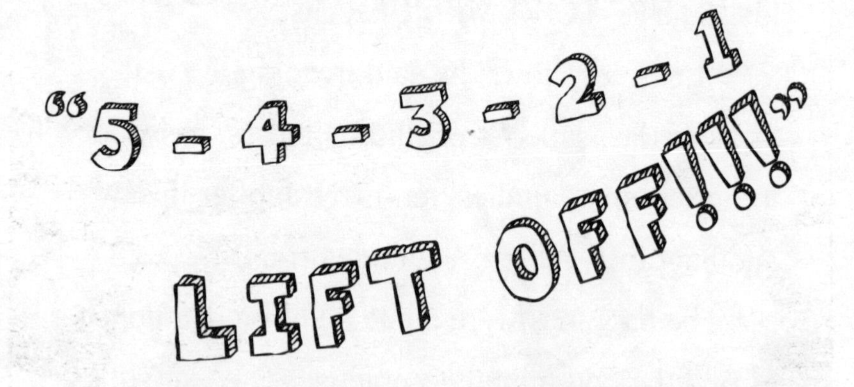

The rocket began to rumble and shake before it zapped upwards towards space. Bob looked determined.

"I'm coming to find you, my friend," he said, quietly. "And I won't go home until I do. I PROMISE!"

Unfortunately, just a minute later, Bob had to break that promise and turn back to Earth, as he wasn't sure if he'd turned the cooker off. Half an hour later though, his rocket was lifting off once again and this time there would be no going back – not even when Bob realised that he hadn't put the bins out.

CHAPTER SIX

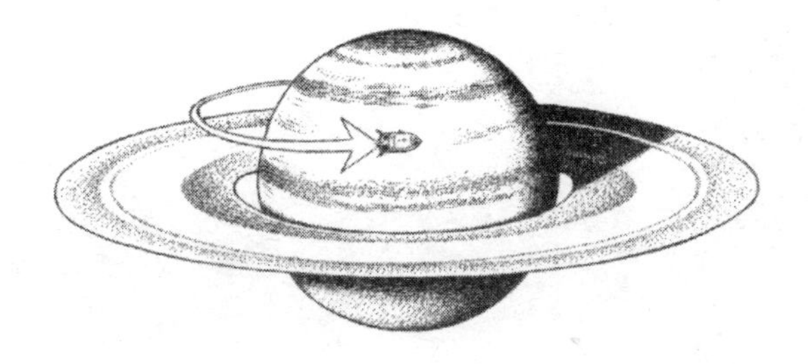

Soon the Earth was just a speck in the rocket's rear-view mirror. Bob began his search with a quick scout round the solar system. First, he swooped sharply left past Mercury and Venus, before doubling back to head for Mars and the outer planets. He carefully counted Jupiter's moons to see if Earth's moon had got mixed up with them.

"Hmmm," he concluded. "Just the usual sixty-three. Come on, Barry. Our moon isn't here!"

Nor was it tucked away in the asteroid belt or in the ice and rocks that made up Saturn's spectacular ring and there was no sign of it shooting around space with Halley's Comet.

That night Bob curled up on the cockpit floor inside his cosy phases-of-the-Moon sleeping bag. Barry dozed in the toolbox. The next day they would circle the Sun.

Bob wasn't fond of the heat. He'd always preferred building snowmen to sandcastles and he had no time for sunbathing.

"Sizzling is for sausages," he would say, "not spacemen!"

But, if the Moon had drifted towards the Sun, it could be in serious danger of melting or cracking. So, after an early flask of tea, they popped on their shades and sped off.

The closer they got to the Sun the hotter it became. Bob stripped down to just his football socks and woollen underpants.

"Phew! You could fry an egg on my forehead!" he gasped, mopping his brow with a fish-paste sandwich.

To cool Barry down, Bob thought about shaving his fur off for him, but, in the end, decided against it.

"We don't want you to look odd, do we?" he said. Barry waggled his eyestalk in agreement and the search continued.

Sadly, they didn't find the Moon and so, with heavy hearts, they swept away from the Sun and into the third day of the hunt.

It was a perilous period of the voyage. Time after time, Bob had to swerve to avoid colliding with cosmic junk left by untidy astronauts. Floating amongst the debris were two rolled up carpets and an old lawn mower. There was a stuffed zebra and a shopping trolley wheel. There were Cola cans and crisp packets and apple cores. And there were hundreds of paint pots and the odd paint brush too.

Strange, thought Bob. *Perhaps they're giving the old space station a makeover. I suppose it could use a lick of paint.*

Later though, when he flew past, the space station was still battleship grey and the graffiti was plain to see.
The Moon, however,
was nowhere.

Bob was worried. In only a few days his job as Man on the Moon would be over. Added to that, space radio reports said that the Moon's disappearance was now raising other worries on Earth. Scientists were wondering how the tides would know when to go in and out. In Paris, fewer people were falling in love without the Moon's romantic glow. And one man in London, who claimed to be a werewolf, said he had no idea which day of the month he should turn hairy and scary. Now Bob realised that it wasn't just his problem. It was the whole world's problem and the weight of that world was on his shoulders. He had to find the Moon – for *everyone*.

But time was rapidly running out and so Bob worked through lunch and cut out sleep. His bagpipes remained silent by the mini-fridge.

On the fourth day Bob and Barry followed the spirally arm of the Milky Way. First one way, then the other. There were countless other galaxies to get through too. Not all were spirally. Some were elliptical like an egg. Some had no shape at all.

On the fifth day they ventured into the far reaches of the universe. They checked every nook and cranny of every black hole. They discovered stars and planets that they never knew existed. They even took a quick peek into the odd parallel universe. Their search was in vain.

By the sixth day Bob and Barry were exhausted. Bob longed for his armchair and slippers. Barry longed for his rubber duck. Before long, their tiredness overcame them and together they nodded off and dreamed of happiness. But not for long. They were rudely awoken when their rocket ground sharply to a halt. There seemed to be no way forward. Bob looked through the porthole. Space was mouse quiet. Not a single star twinkled. There was nothing to see. Nothing that is, except a very small sign. It was a traffic sign. Bob dug out his super-strength binoculars and, as he read aloud, all became clear:

At first Bob was heartbroken.

"It's over," he cried. "We'll never find the Moon now."

As the sign requested, he pulled the rocket's 'reverse' lever to back away from the edge of the universe. And that's when the idea PINGED into his head.

"PLEASE REVERSE!" he shouted. "PLEASE REVERSE. OF COURSE! All we have to do is ask the Stupendous Alacazamo to please reverse his trick and magic the Moon back. It's so simple. Why didn't we think of it earlier?"

So in a super-pacey whoosh they turned around and hurtled for home. When the Earth appeared they were delighted, though also sad not to have the Moon in tow.

"Don't worry Barry old pal," cheered Bob. "When we find the Stupendous Alacazamo our troubles will be over at last! Mark my words."

CHAPTER SEVEN

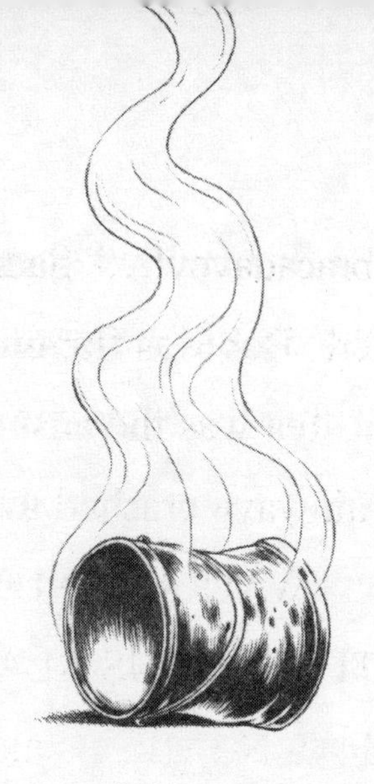

Unfortunately, finding the Stupendous Alacazamo wasn't going to be simple. His tour was over and he too had disappeared from the face of the Earth.

"Where could he be?" wondered Bob.

He looked for clues in the magician's biography, *The Hocus Pocus Hombre*. He searched the city, looking in every bowling alley, bingo hall and chip shop. No luck.

Back at home, Bob flicked to the 'MAGICIAN' section of the telephone directory and slowly thumbed down.

"Let's see: The Sensational What-A-Conno!... The Splendid Shazazamo!... The Tremendous

Abracadavey!…" Sadly, the important name wasn't there. Bob was flummoxed. "What now?" he asked.

Tea was the answer and sure enough a brainwave crashed to shore in Bob's head.

"WAIT A MINUTE!" he shouted, "THE STUPENDOUS ALACAZAMO ISN'T HIS REAL NAME! It said so in *The Hocus Pocus Hombre*. Now what *was* his real name? R… Roger?… No… R…" he flicked though the book. "R… R… Reginald? REGINALD STOPCOCK! THAT'S IT!" Bob grabbed the telephone directory again and found, "Reginald M. Stopcock – BINGO!!"

Ten minutes later Bob knocked on the door of Flat 2, 34 Chilblain Lane, above the 'ABRA-KEBAB-RA' takeaway.

"Hmmm," noted Bob, "not quite the swish, upmarket pad I was expecting!"

The magician's mother, Bertha Stopcock, showed Bob into the living room where the Stupendous Alacazamo was sitting watching horse-racing on television and eating sardines from a tin. He looked different to how had he looked on stage. He was wearing a grubby vest with tatty jogging bottoms, and his brilliant moustache was drooping into stubble so thick, it was almost a beard.

He didn't take his eyes away from the television as Bob nervously talked of tides and Paris and all the trouble caused by the disappearance of the Moon.

"You cannot undo magic," the Stupendous Alacazamo said, grumpily. "And a magician should never discuss his work, so buzz off before I disappear you too!"

Now Bob was really down in the dumps. Not only was the Moon missing but also the Stupendous Alacazamo had turned out to be a ghastly so-and-so.

Back at home, Bob sat at the kitchen table, pondering his next move. As the minutes passed his eyelids became heavy and his head began to loll. He nodded off, dribbling and dreaming, and Barry was soon snoozing too.

Suddenly, they were woken by an almighty crash. Bob and Barry sat bolt upright! Something had hit the house. They ran outside. There was a large dent in the brickwork above the door and, on the ground below, there was a smouldering burnt object. It looked like one of the empty paint pots that had been floating around space.

"How very odd!" Bob remarked, as Barry sniffed around it and singed his nose.

Just then, another smouldering paint pot whizzed down and knocked the head off Bob's favourite garden gnome. *What on earth was going on?* Carefully Bob scanned the night for more plummeting paint pots. His eyes moved slowly until they were distracted by something most strange. There in the sky, around about where crater 367 of the Moon used to be, was a small patch of gold, shimmering and glimmering. It was so beautiful, Bob couldn't take his eyes off it. It was as if the little patch of golden light was calling to him

'WHAT *IS* THAT?' he wondered.

Before he could find out though, a third paint pot shot down and smacked him on the side of the head, knocking him to the crazy paving.

"CRUMBS ALIVE! That smarted a bit!" he moaned, before groggily dragging himself back to his feet.

Half expecting to be crocked once more, Bob plucked up the courage to look upwards again. He couldn't see the golden patch any longer. A blanket of cloud had invaded the sky.

"Barry, do you think I imagined it all?" Bob asked. Barry shrugged.

There was only one way to find out and so, in the blink of an eye, they were again rocketing upwards to where the Moon had once shone.

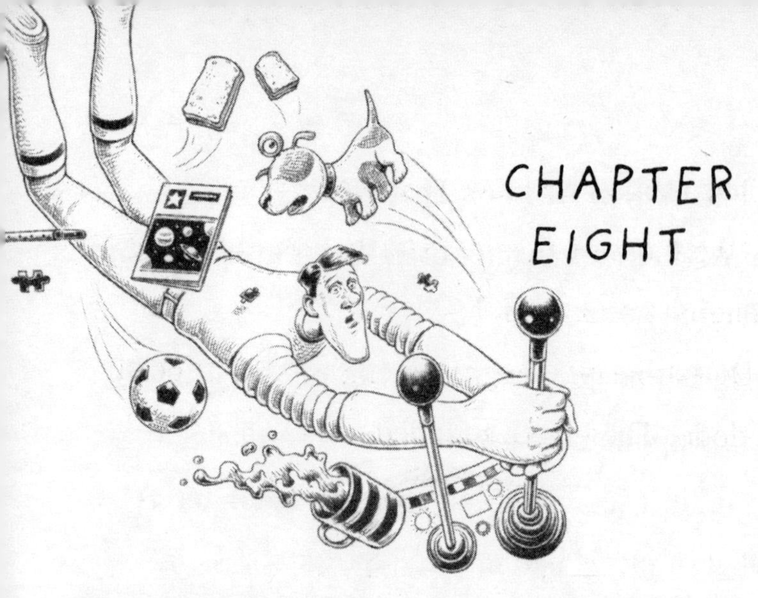

CHAPTER EIGHT

Somehow Bob knew that the golden patch was going to be important.

"We'll soon see, Barry," he said.

First though, they were in for a nasty surprise. As they reached the part of space where the Moon had once been, their rocket suddenly hit something. Bob bravely struggled to keep control as everything outside the window went black and the rocket rattled and scraped and bumped and clattered along, until it finally jarred to a halt. Everything was dark and then the emergency lights came on.

"What the Dickens happened there?" bellowed Bob. "It's as if we hit something invisible."

The rocket was now as still as a pond.

"We must be floating, Barry. I've got to get the engine going again!"

Disastrously, though, the engine was as dead as a dodo. They were stranded.

Bob looked through the porthole window. Even the stars seemed to have been extinguished.

"Maybe we've been sucked into a powerful black hole. Or perhaps we're in some kind of alternative universe dimension thingy!"

There was only one way to find out. "Come on, Barry," Bob called. "Walkies!"

Carefully, Bob opened the hatch of the rocket and he and Barry stepped out into pitch blackness.

Strangely, instead of experiencing the usual space-walk floatiness, their feet made contact with something very solid.

"Huh?" grunted Bob, as he flicked on his torch and began to investigate. Then, "I DON'T BELIEVE IT!" he exclaimed.

They seemed to be in some kind of underground tunnel which twisted away in front of them. But where did it lead? And what kind of ground was it under? The broken-down rocket had blocked the way behind them.

"Well," Bob said, "that only leaves one choice."

So having locked the rocket, Bob set off down the tunnel with Barry, cleverly leaving a trail of dry-roasted peanuts so that they'd be able to find their way back again. They marched for what seemed like an age, until the tunnel began to fork off in all directions. They stopped for a fish-paste sandwich, picked a route and continued.

After a while they were both feeling quite out of puff and, more worryingly, even though it was family-size, the bag of peanuts was almost empty.

Bob was seriously considering turning back to radio for help when, as the tunnel swept to the left, a circle of golden light appeared. Together Bob and Barry walked on until they could see what was what.

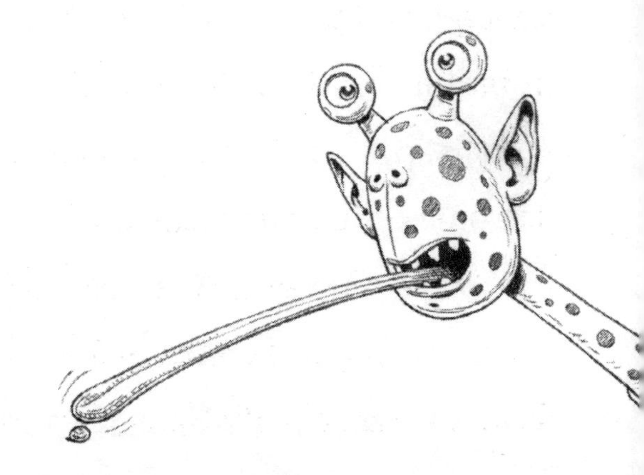

"It's a hole in the rock! A way out!" shouted Bob, nervously. "Hmm, but what if it leads to danger and stuff?" he worried.

He looked for the nut trail. IT WAS GONE!!! *Who had eaten the nuts?*

"BARRY!!" Bob snapped. "YOU GREEDY-GUTS!"

Poor Barry looked confused. He didn't even like dry-roasted peanuts.

Now they had no choice but to investigate the hole, so Bob reached into his astrosuit's backpack and pulled out a rope with a hook on the end of it. Skilfully, he tossed it upwards and the hook snagged on the lip of the hole. With Barry carefully balanced on his helmet, Bob began to climb up.

It was hard work. The closer he got to top of the hole, the brighter the golden glow seemed to be. He continued to heave and pull until he saw something that took his breath away. There were some words carved on the inside rim of the hole:

THEY WERE *HIS* WORDS! He'd spent ages carving them on the inside of crater 367 to mark the passing of the trillennium.

"Huh?" Bob grunted. He was now very confused. There was only one thing to do and so, with a final almighty heave, he pulled himself and Barry up and out of the hole. Looking around him, Bob couldn't believe what he saw…

IT WAS THE MOON! He recognised every rock, every crater, and every scrap of Moon dust he could see. They had just climbed their way up and out of crater 367. He was overjoyed. HE WAS STANDING ON THE MOON.

At least, Bob was standing on a *piece* of the Moon – a small perfect chunk that seemed to be suspended in space like a gigantic biscuit. It was the golden patch he'd seen from his garden. It was very strange. But to have even just a small chunk of Moon back felt glorious and he danced with joy.

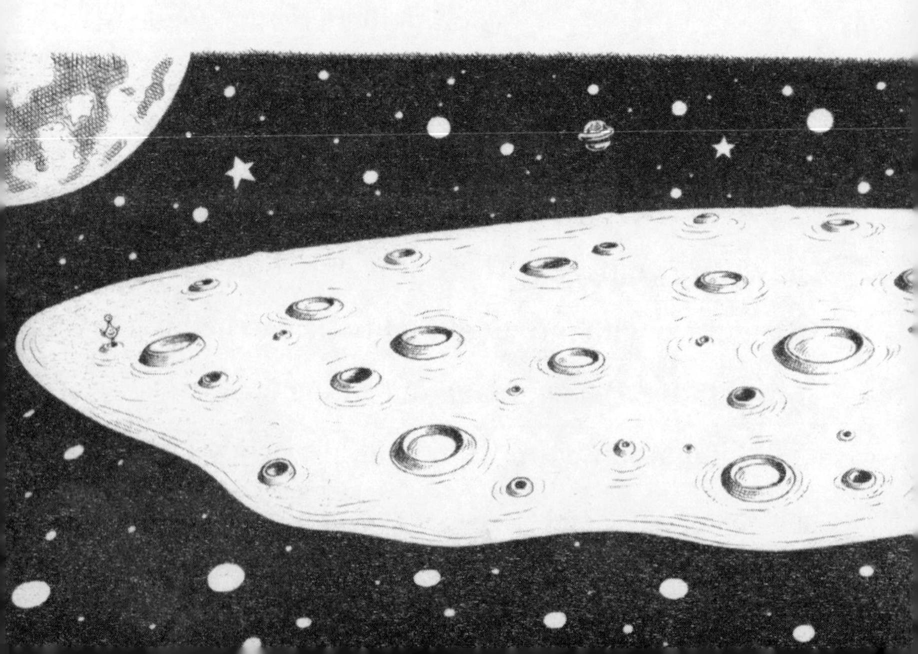

Barry was full of beans too. He was darting here there and everywhere.

"WATCH OUT," cried Bob. "YOU'LL FALL OFF THE EDGE OF THE MOON CHUNK IF YOU'RE NOT CAREFUL!"

Indeed, Barry couldn't stop himself and pelted pell-mell right over the edge of the Moon-chunk. But he didn't plummet downwards or float away. He just kept on running on some kind of invisible surface! Bob's jaw dropped.

"How is he doing that?"

He watched dumbfounded as Barry leapt and bounded on the nothingness. Then, as Barry turned and trotted back onto the Moon-chunk the pitter-patter of his paws left dark, space-coloured prints on the golden surface.

Bob was puzzled. He slowly walked to the edge of the Moon-chunk and stuck out his foot, as if dipping his toes into the sea. His eyes widened to the size of saucers. The darkness

beyond the Moon-chunk edge was solid! Cautiously, he stepped onto it. He stamped his feet. He jumped up and down. The Moon-chunk and what lay beyond it were one and the same thing! Excitedly, Bob bounced between the two and then noticed that, like Barry, he was leaving dark blue footprints on the golden side.

He reached down, touched the sole of his boot and then studied his fingers. They were covered in… PAINT!!! Dark blue paint! Suddenly, he understood everything.

"THAT'S HOW THE STUPENDOUS ALACAZAMO DID IT!" Bob exclaimed. "He painted the moon to camouflage it against the spacescape! He must have run out of paint and had to leave this chunk unfinished!" A tear of relief glistened in his eye. "I CAN'T BELIEVE IT!" he cheered. "THE MOON'S BEEN HERE ALL THE TIME!!!"

CHAPTER NINE

Bob would later learn that while the whole town had been enjoying the magic show, the Stupendous Alacazamo's men were painting the Moon. Slowly, under a layer of dark blue (and silvery dots for the stars) it had *disappeared*, blending perfectly into the cosmic background.

Now the world had to hear of Bob's discovery, so he rushed back to his rocket, thankfully without the aid of dry-roasted peanuts. The map of the Moon was imprinted on his brain. He calculated that his rocket had flown into crater 173 and rattled along a tunnel until it ended up deep underneath the Moon's surface, where the stars didn't shine.

Just minutes later, Bob was giving his rocket a thorough once-over.

"AHA!!!" he smiled. "There's a hairline crack in the engine-booster whatchamacallit. No problemo. Easily fixed!"

And in no time, with the engine-booster whatchamacallit all sticky-taped up, Bob carefully blasted his way up and out of crater 173.

"WE'RE BACK IN BUSINESS," he bellowed. "NEXT STOP, INFINITY HOUSE!!" – via, of course, Vera Crumble's bakery.

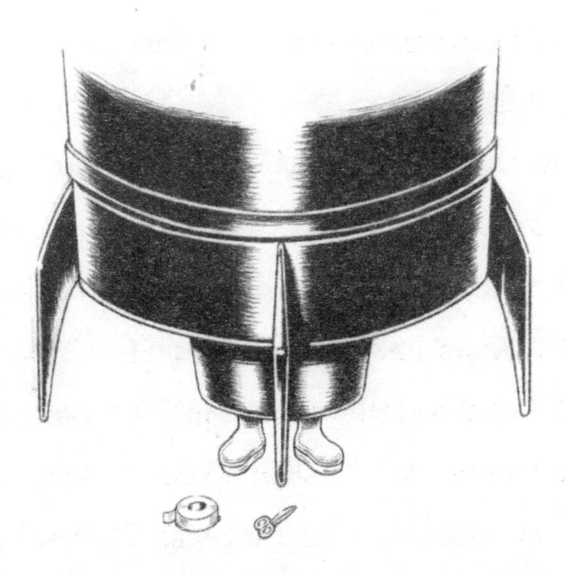

However, back on Earth, Tarantula von Trumpet was unimpressed with Bob's news.

"I'll believe it when I see it," he said, still doodling skulls. "If the whole of the Moon is visible in the sky at midnight tonight, then everything returns to normal. If not, you're finished as the Man on the Moon. Now, please leave cake and shut the door on the way out. Good afternoon!"

Bob was downhearted as he left behind a delicious lemon drizzle cake and made his way out onto the street.

"How can I make the Moon reappear?" he thought. "I *have* to crank my brain up to 'FULL POWER'. I need tea… and fast."

So, at the Moon-Soup Pit-Stop Café, he supped cup after cup until his insides were sloshing and then… "EUREKA!" He knew what had to be done.

Along with Barry, Bob rushed to the Lunar Hill launch-pad and zoomed high into the sky. But they were not heading up to space. Instead, they jetted across the towns and cities of the world stopping off in every hardware shop and DIY superstore they could find. They filled the rocket with jumbo bottles of turpentine paint remover, before popping home.

There, Bob dashed upstairs to his wardrobe and pulled out his Stupendous Alacazamo t-shirt.

Time was rapidly running out. Bob and Barry had only four hours to save his job. There wasn't a moment to spare.

And so, after watching a documentary about onions and trimming his nose hair, Bob took off towards the Moon, being careful not to crash into the invisible bit.

On landing, he took a deep breath. He doused the Stupendous Alacazamo t-shirt in turpentine and ripped it in two, passing half to Barry. It was already nine o'clock.

"Right then," he said, "three hours to go and counting! LET'S GET CLEANING!!!"

And so with elbow grease and snout power they scrubbed and scrubbed until the fruits of their labour began to show. Slowly, more and more paint was removed and eventually, as if by magic, THE MOON BEGAN TO REAPPEAR!!!

CHAPTER TEN

At 9.46 p.m. in Bob's hometown, little Billy Cake noticed something in the sky.

"What's that, Dad?" he asked.

His dad wasn't sure. "If I didn't know better," he said, "I'd swear it was a tiny sliver of Moon!"

At 10.34 p.m., on spotting the slowly-growing crescent, Hyacinth Trombone almost crashed her moped into the river.

And at 11.21 p.m., the open-air concert by Gordon and the Little Green Men was halted mid-encore when Gordon spied the three-quarter glow above the stage.

"IT'S A MIRACLE!!" shouted Alfie Bean.

"IT'S MAGIC!" cheered Emily St Bernard.

"IT CAN'T BE HAPPENING!" cried the Stupendous Alacazamo.

Word spread like wildfire. Newspapers changed their headlines. Radio stations cancelled all music to keep listeners updated. And every TV camera in the world was pointing one way – UPWARDS. By now, everyone had heard about Bob and Barry's midnight deadline and they all watched the sky with bated breath as the Moon slowly reappeared.

"COME ON, LADS!! Come on!!" cried Davey Cup at 11.51 p.m.

"YOU CAN DO IT, BOYS!" roared Bella Tremlett-Brown at 11.56 p.m.

"YOU'RE NEARLY THERE!!" screamed Royston Blackbird at 11.59 p.m.

With only a minute to go till midnight there was only a hair's breadth to scrub. The crowd fell silent. Some couldn't watch. Some held hands. But everyone wished with all their hearts. They wished for the moon.

And then at 11.59 and 59 seconds, the news was announced.

"IT'S OFFICIAL," reported Clint Powerman of SBTV. "THE WHOLE OF THE MOON… I REPEAT… THE WHOLE OF THE MOON HAS RETURNED! IT GIVES ME GREAT PLEASURE TO CONFIRM THAT THE MOON IS BACK!!!"

Huge roars filled the air. Streamers flew. Strangers hugged. The Earth danced.

In Paris, Jean-Claude Petit-Pois noticed Isabel Poulet across a crowded boulevard and his heart missed a beat.

In London, Walter Poodle combed his fur and cleaned his razor-sharp teeth before popping out for a late-night steak.

And on the seventeenth floor of Infinity House, Tarantula von Trumpet, stopped doodling skulls, looked up and smiled.

"Good lad, Bob," he said. "Good lad."

Fifteen minutes later, Bob's rocket could be seen heading back to Earth. Thousands had gathered at the Lunar Hill launch-pad to get a glimpse of their new heroes!

When Bob and Barry finally clambered out of the hatch, the noise was deafening. They were both space-coloured from head to foot and looked completely and utterly exhausted. Even so, they were proud and they were happy.

They couldn't believe the celebrations that were taking place in front of them. As a reward, for their work, the mayor presented both of them with a makeshift trophy and, even though it had

a statue of a snooker player on it, Bob was delighted. It was the thought that counted and the thought was good.

Clint Powerman was the first journalist to arrive on the scene.

"It's been reported," he said, "that you were within a second of losing your job as Man on the Moon. How does it feel to have saved it?"

"Not bad, Clint," replied Bob. "Not bad at all.

But do you know what feels even better than that?"

"No, Bob. Tell me!" said Clint.

"SAVING THE MOON ITSELF!!" said Bob. "It's absolutely true what they say – YOU DON'T KNOW WHAT YOU'VE GOT TILL IT'S GONE! Now, it's been a long week and so, if you don't mind, I'm going to nip off home for

a bath and a beef-paste sandwich. Then Barry and I need to rest. There's one heck of a lot of Moon work to catch up on!!! GOODNIGHT ALL!"

Once again the crowd cheered and clapped and roared. Only one single, solitary "BOO!" struggled to be heard and it came from the mouth of the Stupendous Alacazamo. His protest, however, soon ended when a paint pot fizzed down from the sky and

bopped him on the bonce, knocking him out good and proper.

As Bob cycled away he was still wearing his filthy space suit. With an equally scruffy Barry balanced on his head, he waved his snooker trophy aloft and slowly disappeared into the distance, often gazing upwards to make sure the Moon was still there.

At home he had a beef-paste sandwich and Barry had a selection of bones. Then after a thoroughly good bath they wandered into their garden to enjoy the night.

Bob picked up his bagpipes and he played like he never had before. And even though cats scarpered and owls fainted, the music must have been as sweet as sugar because, high in the sky, the golden Moon was smiling, and when the Moon smiled it meant everything was going to be alright.

THE END?

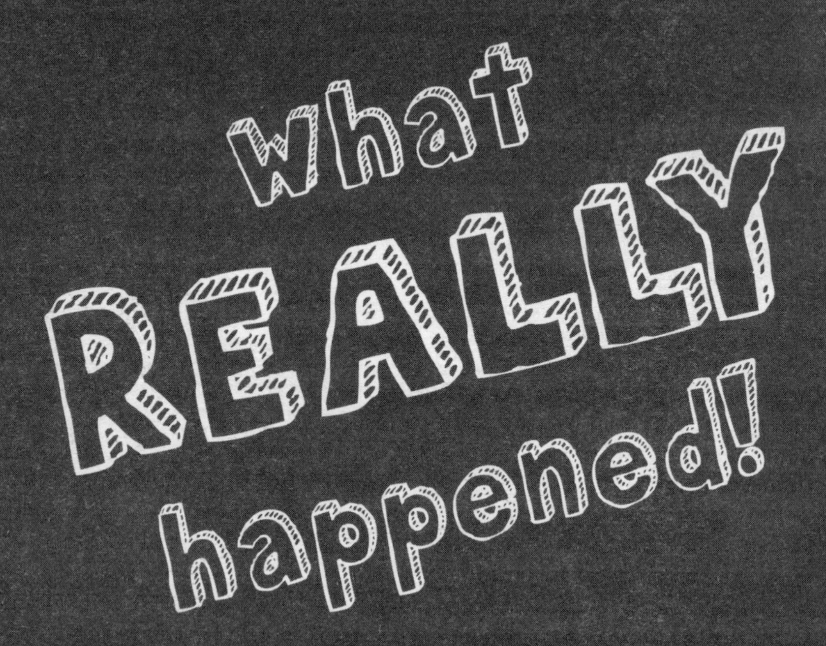

FRIDAY 7TH MARCH
20:30

Back on Earth Alacazamo is entertaining the crowds with his magic show. Meanwhile...

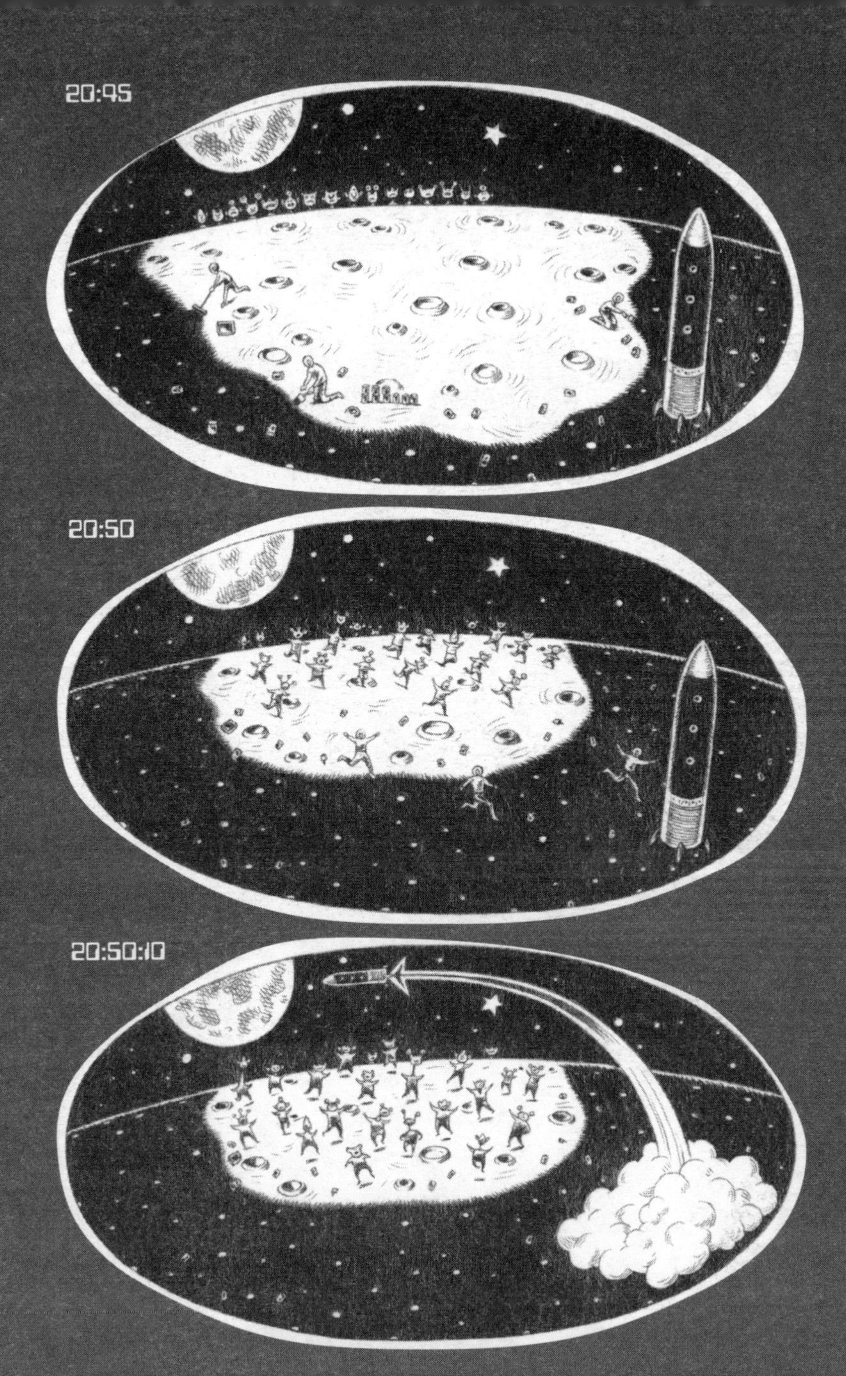
20:45
20:50
20:50:10

THE END